Through The
Witch's Window

Through The Witch's Window

Hazel Townson

Illustrated by Tony Ross

A Red Fox Read-Alone Book

A Red Fox Book
Published by Arrow Books Limited
20 Vauxhall Bridge Road, London SW1V 2SA

An imprint of the Random Century Group
London Melbourne Sydney Auckland
Johannesburg and agencies throughout the world

First published in Great Britain in hardback in 1989
by Andersen Press Ltd

Red Fox edition 1990
Reprinted 1990

Text © Hazel Townson 1989
Illustrations © Andersen Press Ltd 1989

Made and printed in Great Britain by
The Guernsey Press Co Ltd
Guernsey, C.I.

ISBN 0 09 966860 2

*For the staff and pupils of my
grandchildren's school,
Heaton Park Primary,
Whitefield*

Chapter One

Thud, crash, tinkle!
Once upon a time there was a
broken window.

With a hole in it shaped like a Big,
Black Star.

Who broke it?
Lily Dollop, kicking her brother
Danny's football.
What did Lily do?

She ran away. Fast.
Because Granny Gowie, who lived
in the house, was said to be a bit
of a witch.

(How can you be a *bit* of a witch?
Which bit is the witch bit?
The pointed hat? The big, bent
nose? The evil grin? The long,
skinny fingers?)

Lily Dollop ran all the way home.
But it didn't do her any good,
because the Big, Black Star out of
Granny Gowie's window came
after her.

'Ah, go on! It couldn't have!' you
will say.

But you don't know Granny
Gowie. She can turn toads into
stools and mush into rooms.
You should have seen that Big,
Black Star whizzing through the
air like a spiky frisbee!

All the birds flew out of its way.
Except one greedy pigeon, who
was too busy gobbling burnt toast
on the top of a telephone box.

The Big, Black Star speared that
pigeon like a chip on a fork.

It was lucky the Star caught on a telly-aerial and spun right round, so the pigeon fell off again.

But it was a near thing, and one of the pigeon's feathers stuck to the Star.
So there was this Big, Black Star with a feather in its cap, coming after Lily Dollop down Upping Street.

Will it catch up with her?
Read Chapter Two to find out.

Chapter Two

Lily Dollop lolloped home.
She was so out of breath she could
not speak.
'Where have you been?' asked Mrs
Dollop. 'Your tea's ready.'

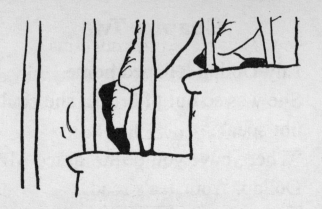

But Lily didn't want any tea,
although it was sausage and chips.
Lily ran straight upstairs and
locked her bedroom door.
'You come down this minute!'
shouted Mrs Dollop.

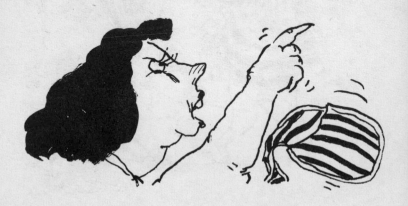

But Lily closed the curtains,
jumped into bed with everything
on except her shoes, and pulled
the blankets over her head.
She was expecting trouble.

'Our Lily won't eat her tea,' Mrs Dollop complained to Mr Dollop. 'You don't eat tea, you drink it,' joked Mr Dollop.

He was the life and soul of the
Sardine Canning Factory, and
would not have believed in the
Big, Black Star if it had dropped
on the table like a splat of treacle.

'*I'll* eat Lily's sausage and chips,'
said Danny Dollop. 'I'm hungry.
I've trudged miles looking for my
football. I think somebody's
pinched it.'
By now, the Big, Black Star was
whizzing over Lily Dollop's fence.

It made a muffled whirring noise,
like a washing-machine with a vest
stuck in the works.
Lily could hear it, even through
the blankets.
She shook so much with fright
that her bed did a samba right
across the room.

'What's that girl up to now?' cried Mrs Dollop.
'She's up to page 29 in her reading book,' said Danny.

Did Danny get a clip on the ear
for being cheeky?
Read Chapter Three to find out.

Chapter Three

'Cheeky!' cried Mrs Dollop to Danny.

'You just go and fetch your sister down here this very second!'

'Can't!' said Danny. 'I'm here this very second. By the time I get upstairs it will be ten seconds later.'

But he went.
Danny tapped on Lily's door.
'It's me!'
But Lily could not hear him
because the blankets were pulled
over her head.

Lily was saying her prayers.
'Please save me from Granny
Gowie, and I'll never play football
again!' she prayed. 'The only
things I'll kick in future will be
boys who pull my hair.'
Meantime, out on the
landing . . .

'What's that muffled whirring noise?' wondered Danny, feeling a breeze round his ankles.

Before he could answer himself,
the Big, Black Star had already
whirled its way up the stairs and
posted itself under Lily's bedroom
door like a Letter of Doom.

Was Danny too late to save his sister?
Read Chapter Four to find out.

Chapter Four

The Big, Black Star whirled all
round Lily Dollop's bedroom.
It set the lampshade spinning and
the curtains doing curtsies.
It flicked the fingers of the clock
right round to midnight, which
was Granny Gowie's witching
hour.

Then it tweaked the blankets from
the bottom of the bed and tickled
Lily's feet with its pigeon feather.

Lily Dollop could not stand having
her feet tickled.
She thrashed about in bed like a
trout on a line.

She shrieked so loudly that her
mum and dad came running.
'What's to do?' cried Mrs Dollop,
banging on the wood.
'Open this door at once!' cried Mr
Dollop.

'I'll bet it's all her teacher's fault,' guessed Danny. 'Our Lily always said she'd have a fit if Mrs Slice was nice to her.'

'Well, if Lily's having a fit I'm going to break the door down,' said Mr Dollop.

He moved backwards across the
landing to take a good run at the
door . . .

. . .and fell down the stairs!
Bump—bump—yell—bump—
bump—BUMP—silence!

Did Mr Dollop kill himself, or
didn't he?
Read Chapter Five to find out.

Chapter Five

Mr Dollop banged his head on the bottom step and knocked himself out.

'Fred!' cried Mrs Dollop, rushing to his side.

'Well, don't just stand there!' she called to Danny. 'Fetch a drink or something.'
So Danny ran off to the kitchen.

He thought a drink was a silly idea
when his dad was unconscious, so
he brought the first Something he
came to, which was a cheese
grater.

Meantime, Lily was shrieking fit to split.

Lily had leapt out of bed and was dancing round the room like a speeded-up ballerina, trying to keep her feet away from the fatal feather.

Lily had always been quick on her
feet, but she had never danced a
step before, except across a
football field.

She was amazed at how easily the ballet steps came to her.
She danced and danced, and the Big, Black Star danced after her, down near the carpet, trying to push its feather under her feet to drive Lily stark, staring mad.

Round and round the room they
went, knocking things over,
making a terrible row.
Lily had a radio by her bed, and at
one point, with one point, the Star
turned it on.

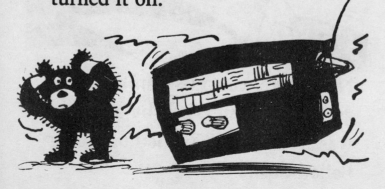

Now there was music in the room
as well as clatter, and by all that
was wonderful it turned out to be
ballet music!

Lily danced faster and faster.
Will that girl ever stop dancing?
Read Chapter Six to find out.

Danny Dollop's dad came round.
He shook himself and felt the top
of his head.

It had a bump on it the size of a
Bath bun.
'Put some butter on it,' said Mrs
Dollop.

So they all went into the kitchen.
Whilst they were bustling about
there, buttering Mr Dollop's head,
a foot came through the ceiling.

'That's our Lily's foot!' cried Mrs
Dollop, dropping the butter-pot on
Mr Dollop's head and knocking
him out again.

(How did she know it was Lily's foot?
Mothers have an instinct for these things, and anyway Lily's bedroom was right overhead.)

Mrs Dollop made a hurricane of
her voice.
'You take your foot out of that
ceiling or you'll be in big trouble!
Just wait till your dad comes
round.'

Lily knew that Force Ten voice. It
had to be obeyed.

So she yanked her foot out of the
hole with all her might—and
kicked the Big, Black Star right in
its middle.

The Big, Black Star saw stars.
It went whizzing through the
window before you could say
'Milky Way', and dived down into
the deadly depths of the poisoned
canal.

On its way out, of course, it broke
Lily's window . . .

. . . and left behind a hole
shaped like a Big, Black Star with
a pigeon feather stuck to the top of
it.

Lily Dollop never did stop
dancing.
She went into pantomime, then

television, then the Royal Ballet.
Her ambition knew no bounds, or
leaps either.

'Star-struck, that's what she is!'
sighed Mrs Dollop fondly.
And her butter-struck husband
had to agree.

Did Danny Dollop ever get his
football back?
Well, what do *you* think?